Sad Rocky

Illustrated by The Artful Doodlers

Random House New York
Thomas the Tank Engine & Friends™

CREATED BY BRITT ALLCROFT

Based on The Railway Series by The Reverend W Awdry. © 2010 Gullane (Thomas) LLC.
Thomas the Tank Engine & Friends and Thomas & Friends are trademarks of Gullane (Thomas) Limited.
HIT and the HIT Entertainment logo are trademarks of HIT Entertainment Limited.
All rights reserved. Published in the United States by Random House Children's Books, a division of Random House, Inc., 1745 Broadway, New York, NY 10019, and in Canada by Random House of Canada Limited, Toronto. Step into Reading, Random House, and the Random House colophon are registered trademarks of Random House, Inc.
www.stepintoreading.com   www.randomhouse.com/kids   www.thomasandfriends.com

Educators and librarians, for a variety of teaching tools, visit us at
www.randomhouse.com/teachers
ISBN: 978-0-375-85368-5   MANUFACTURED IN CHINA

HiT entertainment

Where is Gordon?

Where is James?

They are in the shed.

Where is Rocky?

He is in the sun.

He can not fit in the shed.

Rocky is sad.

He is not like James.

He is not like Gordon.

Rocky wants to fit
in the shed, too.
"You can not fit!"
says Gordon.
"You have a hook."

Sad Rocky runs and hides.

"I can not fit in,"

says Rocky.

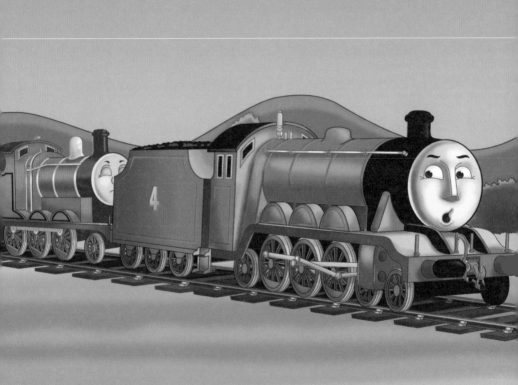

Look!

James has hit Gordon.

They want help.

Where is Rocky?

Rocky wants to help.

He is happy he has a hook!

James and Gordon are happy, too.

Rocky does not fit in the shed.

Rocky does fit as a friend.